DETROIT CITY GIRLS

Kita Cochran

ISBN-13: 9798842065929

Cover design by: Renee Luke Designs; ReneeLuke.net

Printed in the United States of America

DEDICATION

This is dedicated to my family and friends who provide me unconditional love and support.

CONTENTS

INTRODUCTION

Detroit, Michigan has long been a city of grit, innovation, pure hustle, risk-taking, and swagg personified.

History has documented a lot of men in these categories; however, "the streets" have known for many decades that there is a certain segment of Detroit city girls who also fit this description to the max. They have a survival instinct like nobody else.

You push these women, they push back harder. Some *set* the rules - with no apologies. And for those who wonder about the price these women pay, you may never know unless life hands *you* the ultimate challenge. Game on!

CHAPTER 1

Detroit, Michigan

BANG! BANG! BANG!

"Fuuuck!" somebody yelled from the back room.

"Rocko, what was that?" little Rocky asked his older brother.

"Shhh, be quiet, Rock!" Rocko whispered in response. Then, they heard other noises from the back of the house.

"What the fuck?! Oh my God! Roc!" the boys' mother, Sydney, yelled as she moved toward her injured husband. She shoved her best friend Tasha into Omar's arms. Omar was just standing there in shock after shooting his younger brother.

"Give me your phone!" Sydney said to Tasha. "Oh my God!"

She kept her eyes on Roc as she dialed 911.

"Roc, Baby." She knelt down beside him as she felt his weak pulse. "Roc, Baby, don't do this to me. Don't you do this to me! ... Hello?! I need an ambulance to 6 Mile and Freeland," she spoke firmly into the cell phone. "We're the last house off the corner. My husband's been shot, and he's bleeding everywhere."

"Ma'am, what is your name?" the 911 operator asked.

"Sydney Williams."

"And what's your husband's name?"

"Rockail Williams."

"Where was he shot?"

"The chest and leg. And I think the shoulder or arm. There's so much blood, I can't tell."

"Okay, okay. Is he breathing?"

"Yes, but it's very shallow, and ..." She put her ear to his chest. "I can't tell if there's bubbling in his lungs, but I think I'm losing him!" She noticed his gun was still lying next to him.

"Please hurry!"

She ended the call and tore a strip off the bottom of her dress and tied it around his arm as tight as she could. Then she tore another strip off and tied it around his leg. "Roc, if you can hear me, I love you, Baby, and you're a fighter. I need you to fight. Fight for me, Baby. Fight for me and our boys. We need you, Baby. I can't do this without you. Don't make me do this without you. Do you hear me, Roc?"

I hear you, Baby. Roc was talking to her, but no words were coming out of his mouth. He felt as if he was slowly falling to sleep.

The boys ran to the back room, shocked to see their mom covered in blood and kneeling beside their father.

"Get my babies outta here! They can't see this!" Syndney said.

Tasha tried to run past Omar, but he grabbed her by the arm. "Bitch! Where is you going?"

"Please, Omar, don't do this!" Sydney yelled.

"Fuck that, Bitch! Get up and get my money," he said, committed to completing his robbery of his half-brother despite the tragic turn of events.

"Okay, Omar, just don't hurt my boys." Sydney slowly got up and walked towards the back closet with Omar.

"Omar, why are you doing this?" Sydney asked.

"Bitch, shut the fuck up and get my money!"

Sydney opened the door and looked down at the safe on the floor.

"Bitch, get the money outta there!" A minute later, Omar grabbed the two million dollars in cash and ran out the door.

Sydney ran back to Roc, rested his head in her lap, then whispered, "Please, Baby, don't die on me."

There was a loud bang as the front door was kicked in. "Police!" an officer yelled.

"Back here!" Tasha screamed. She then quickly shut the safe and closed the closet door.

The officer moved to the back room and saw the blood pouring from Roc. "Holy shit!" He pressed the talk button on his walkie-talkie and said, "They're here in the back room. There's one victim." To Sydney, the officer asked, "Is there anyone else hurt? Where is the shooter?"

"No, nobody else is hurt. And I don't know where

he went, but he's gone."

The officer was a rookie and had never seen a live and up-close gunshot victim before. "The ambulance is here, Ma'am." Sydney kept crying as the paramedics rushed into the room.

"Ma'am," the older paramedic said, "we need you to step aside. Please." He helped her up as he asked if Roc was her husband.

She nodded *yes* and allowed herself to be helped to her feet.

"Ma'am, we need to stabilize him. You said he was shot, right?"

"Yeah. Three times, I think." She watched as they ripped Roc's clothes off and set up an IV. Soon, he was on the gurney and being led into the back of the ambulance. When Sydney tried to climb up into the back of the ambulance with him, the older paramedic shook his head *no* at her.

"What are you shaking your head for?! That's my husband, and you better believe that I will be riding with him!" She was about to lose it.

"We need to be alone with the victim so we can work on saving his life."

Two of the paramedics worked on Roc as the female paramedic tried to calm Sydney down, but she was holding on tight to the back of the ambulance door.

"You're wasting precious time, Ma'am."

"Fuck you! That's my husband, and I'm not leaving him!"

"Ma'am, what's happening?" the officer asked.

"My husband may be dying, and these muthafuckas are tryna tell me I can't ride with him! I'm riding!" She climbed up into the back of the ambulance, screaming, "Don't touch me! Don't fucking touch me! I'm going with my husband!"

The paramedic was still trying to grab Sydney when Tasha ran up.

"Tasha, grab my purse and the boys, and meet us at the hospital."

"Which one?"

Sydney looked at the paramedic expectantly.

The paramedic sighed and said, "The one farther down this street, Ma'am."

"Yeah, the one down the street," Sydney repeated and closed the ambulance door.

CHAPTER 2

"Oh, God, please." Sydney closed her eyes and prayed as they went to work on Roc. She hoped that when she opened her eyes, this would all have been a nightmare.

"C'mon, People, we're losing him!" the older paramedic yelled, snapping Sydney back to reality.

"Damn you, Roc. Don't you do this! Don't you die on me!" she cried. "Fight, Baby!" She spoke as if she could actually hear him talking back, saying that he was trying but it burned. "Fight for me and the boys. I need you, Baby. We all need you. You're my world. Don't do this, Roc. I need you to stay with me."

The heart monitor was getting slower, and his vitals were dropping. Sydney didn't want to truly believe that he was dying.

"There's too much blood loss," the female paramedic was saying.

"Is he gonna make it? He's gonna make it, right?" Sydney was grasping for any hope that she could.

"I can't promise you anything, Ma'am. His vitals are dropping fast. Excuse me."

◆ ◆ ◆

Later, at the hospital:

"Mrs. Williams?"

"Yes?" Sydney answered.

"I'm Detective Jones. We have some questions for you. So, let's start at the beginning."

"Me and Roc was out. Tasha was home with the boys."

"Okay. Who is Tasha?"

"That's my best friend."

"Do you know the shooter?"

Sydney thought about it for a minute before answering. "No." She knew the rules of the game: an eye for an eye.

"Ma'am, you do understand that we can't do our job if you don't give us anything?"

"Y'all job is to find the muthafucka that shot my husband, not question me!"

"Mrs. Williams, how can we do our job if you don't let us?"

"If I don't know nothing, how the fuck can I help you?! Is that all?"

"For now."

Shortly after, Sydney looked down the hallway and saw her boys running towards her with tears in their eyes.

"Mom! Mom! What happened with Papa?"

"I don't know yet. Ain't nobody telling me nothing."

"Excuse me. Are you Mrs. Williams?"

"Yes."

"Well, I'm the doctor that performed surgery on your husband. The surgery was a success; however, we had to put him in a medically-induced coma."

"What?! What the fuck did y'all do to my husband?!"

"Mrs. Williams, we had to do it to save his life."

Sydney burst into tears and fell to the floor. "Why, God?!" After a few minutes, they helped her up and she said, "I want to see my husband. Tasha, watch the boys."

"Okay, Sis."

Sydney followed the doctor down the hallway until they reached the room. She entered the sterile room and walked towards Roc's body. Sydney looked at him in shock and turned to the doctor.

"May I be alone with my husband, please?"

"Yes, Ma'am," the doctor said before leaving.

"Damn you, Roc! We need you out here. What am I gonna do without you? I love you, Baby." She took a few moments to compose herself then said, "Okay… okay. I got the boys, so don't worry about nothing. Just get better for us." She spoke for a few more minutes until the hospital staff returned.

"Ma'am, it's time to move him, and we need to go."

"Okay." Sydney leaned down and kissed Roc on the lips. Then, she wiped her eyes before going to meet up with Tasha and the boys.

Weeks went by, and Sydney was still in disbelief that Roc was in a coma.

"Damn, this shit can't be real. What am I gonna do?" she cried out for Roc.

Minutes later, there was a loud knock at the door. She jumped out of the bed and ran towards the door, irrationally thinking it was Roc. She swung open the door – only to see an older lady standing outside with two bodyguards.

"What do you want?" Sydney asked.

"My name is Ms. Golden, but your husband called me *Goddess*." She smiled slightly then said, "He said my spirit somehow reminded him of his mother even though he was small when she died."

Sydney thought for a minute and remembered an older lady who used to call Roc late at night and he would go meet her. Roc used to say that the lady was gonna change their lives.

Her ethnicity was difficult to pinpoint. Her slight accent, light bronze face and beautiful, naturally curly hair suggested she could have been from the Caribbean, South America or even Europe somewhere. She radiated that sophisticated, continental look.

"Roc's not here," Sydney said.

"I know. He's at the hospital in a coma. I'm not here to see Roc though. I'm here to talk to you."

"What about?"

"Your husband and I had business, and I'm out of two million dollars."

At that moment, Sydney was focused on the bodyguards in the room. "Well, I can't help you."

"Don't worry, Sydney. We know Omar took the money, but business is business, and our business must continue."

"Look, I don't want anything to do with Rockail's business."

"I wish things were that simple, but they're not. So, we're going to supply you with twenty-five kilos every month. And relax, this is good for you and the boys."

"I don't know the first thing about selling drugs."

"We'll teach you."

"Teach me?! Are you crazy?"

"Roc said from the beginning that you were smarter than him. He was very clear that if anything happened to him, you would take over. We're going to set up your operation, and you're going to have one of the biggest drug rings in the Midwest. It'll be worth millions."

"I can't get caught up in this, because I won't leave my boys."

"You won't, if you are indeed smart. Bolo." One of the large bodyguards started walking towards Sydney holding a duffle bag.

"Give the woman her bag," Goddess said.

"What's this?"

"It's twenty-five keys of one hundred percent pure heroin. You will deal in weight only, no small sells."

◆ ◆ ◆

Later, Sydney sat looking in shock at the bag with the twenty-five keys on the table. She knew there was no denying the responsibility. She couldn't believe Roc would put her in that type of situation though. What could he be thinking about, taking that deal? She rushed to the phone and called Tasha. "Girl, drop the boys off at your mom's house and get over here asap!"

An hour went by before there was a knock at the door. "Thank God it's you."

"Bitch, what is the problem?"

"Did you drop the boys off?"

"Yeah, Girl. Now tell me what the fuck is going on."

"This nigga Roc!"

"Roc? What about him?"

"Girl, this nigga made a deal with some old-ass lady for twenty-five keys. And that two million that Omar took was hers!"

"Wait. What?"

"This lady just left and told me what he owe ... shit, what *I* owe now."

"How the fuck is you gonna come up with two million dollars?"

"She told me how. Grab that bag right there."

"Damn. Bitch, what the fuck is in this heavy ass bag?"

"Her solution." Sydney unzipped the bag.

"Damn. Bitch, do you know what the fuck that is?"

"Yeah. That's the problem."

"Bitch, that ain't the problem; it's the answer."

"Girl, I don't know the first thing about selling dope."

"Bitch, all yo' niggas been drug dealers. What don't you know about selling dope."

"Yeah, but that's their shit, and I stay out of it."

"Now look what that got you. You're still involved."

Sydney just shook her head.

"Bitch, stop looking at this as a problem and start looking at it as an opportunity to get from up under these niggas' boots and be yo' own boss."

"Girl, I just want to make the money Roc owe this lady and get me and my boys out of this shit."

"Yeah, okay."

"I just need you to get at that nigga Pooh for me and see what he paying a key."

"Alright, I'll send him a text to call me." Tasha then sent the text.

"Thank you, Girl, and thanks for always riding with me."

"You my sister 'til death do us part."

"Oh yeah, I need you to tell yo' momma to watch the boys until we figure this shit out."

"Okay. Wait, that nigga Pooh just popped back at me." She hugged Sydney. "We got this. Now let me go see this nigga and see what he talking 'bout."

Sydney was still unsure that things would work out. She was frustrated as she jumped back into bed, thinking about keeping her boys safe. She then started thinking about that nigga Block. He was her boyfriend before Roc, and Roc hated him. Sydney had never loved Block, but she needed a support system and she knew he dealt in weight. She hated that she even needed the nigga. She knew that if Roc ever found out, he would kill Block – and her – but she still called him.

"What up doe? Who dis?"

"Syd."

"Who?"

"Nigga, stop playing. You know who this is!"

"Ha ha. Damn, Baby, long time no hear."

"Yeah, it's been a minute. Look, I want to bump into you."

"Name the time and place, and I'll be there."

"Today. JJ's at five."

"Okay. Can't wait."

She knew that Block was still in love with her, so to seal the deal she was gonna have to make sure he knew she was there on business.

CHAPTER 3

Sydney pulled up to JJ's and saw Block's S550 parked by the door. She parked the black Range Rover that Roc had bought her for Mother's Day. When she walked in, Block noticed her right away because she was still that bitch: beautiful light-golden complexion and thick as hell.

"Damn!" he said. "You still bad as a muthafucka. I missed you."

"Yeah okay, Block."

"I heard your nigga got shot."

"Yeah, he good though."

"That ain't what the streets saying. They saying that nigga on his death bed."

"Look, fuck the streets and what they're saying. Nigga, I'm not here to talk about my husband. I'm here to talk numbers."

"Bitch, what?! Numbers? What type of numbers Little Syd talking about?"

Sydney reached into her purse and pulled out an ounce of heroin.

"Bitch, what the fuck is that?"

"Nigga, you know what it is."

"Okay, so Little Syd is in the dope game."

"Look, Block, I can get you keys of this shit, and it's a hundred percent pure."

Block took a hit off the ounce. "Damn, Syd! This shit is good. Where the fuck you get some shit like this from?"

"That shit don't matter. What do matter is I got it. Okay?"

"Okay, Boss Lady. Let's get down to business. I'm paying sixty-two thousand a key. Can you beat that number?"

"I can give it to you for forty-five a key."

"I need ten keys by tomorrow."

"Okay. Call me when you're ready."

"Damn, Baby, can I get a hug or something from yo' fine ass?"

"Come on, Block, let's keep this shit professional."

"It's all business, Baby."

"Okay." Sydney leaned in for a hug, and Block squeezed her ass. "Damn, Nigga. Why you gotta be disrespectful?"

"My hand slipped," he laughed. After Sydney jumped back into her truck and pulled off, Block asked himself what type of shit she was on. He figured she must've stolen the dope from Roc. *Fuck it,* he thought. *That bitch gonna be my bounce back.* He got into his car, pulled out his phone and called his man LA. "What up doe, Young Nigga?"

"Shit, chilling. What's the word?"

"I got one on the floor."

"Yeah? Who?"

"Roc."

"Ain't that the nigga who just got shot?"

"Yeah, that's him."

"Ain't that nigga dead already?"

"Not him. The play on his bitch."

"A'ight. What's the tag?"

"Hundred."

"Yeah? When?"

"Asap."

"Say less. I'm on it."

When Sydney pulled back up to the house, she saw Tasha waiting on her.

"Where you been?" Tasha asked.

"Pulled up on the fat ass nigga Block. His ass looks like he gained a hundred pounds."

Tasha started laughing.

Sydney said with a smile on her face, "Bitch, that shit ain't funny."

"Girl, a hundred pounds my ass. That nigga a dope head. Why the fuck would you call him and he ain't got no money? He out here getting niggas robbed," Tasha replied.

"Damn. I ain't know he fell off like that."

"These niggas ain't hustlers. They drug addicts. Look, I talked to that nigga Pooh, and he with it. See, that nigga's a real hustler."

"Alright. Set the meet up."

"I'll call you when he ready to meet up."

After Tasha pulled off, Sydney's phone began

ringing. "Hello?"

"Mom, when you coming to get us?"

"Soon, Rocko. Where is your brother?"

"In the room, playing the game."

"Well, I love you boys, and I'll be over there soon."

Sydney was walking towards the house, not knowing that LA was watching her from across the street.

He started walking up to Sydney, creeping on the side of her car. She never saw him running up.

"Oh shit!" she said.

"Bitch, don't move! Open the door!"

Sydney was shook up as she opened the door and dropped the keys on the floor.

"Sit down, Baby." Sydney was crying uncontrollably as she did what she was told. "Chill out; you good. I just want to talk to you," he said.

"You damn sure know how to start a conversation," Sydney responded.

"Look, I don't know you. So, when that fat-ass nigga Block put a hundred thousand on your head, I had to see what for."

"That nigga a snake! I gave him the opportunity to make some real money."

"What was the opportunity?"

"I was gonna flood that nigga with pure heroin for cheap; but, Nigga, fuck all that. If you gonna do it, do it!"

LA started laughing. "Oh, so you a gangsta? I like that. So, where is all this pure dope?"

"I ain't telling you shit!"

"Okay, I get that. Get up! Let's go to the bedroom."

Sydney got up and started walking to the back room. When they got there, LA told her to sit down.

"So, you're not gonna tell me where the dope at? Okay, let's see. Where would I hide my dope? Maybe the closet.... Look at what we got here. I wonder what's in this black duffle bag." LA unzipped the bag and looked at the contents. "Damn, Girl, you're on a mission. Look, I want to offer you a deal."

"What type of deal?"

"The kind of deal where you get to keep all of your dope and you hire me."

CHAPTER 4

After LA left, Sydney started thinking about what he had said. She couldn't believe that Block wanted to put a hit out on her. Damn, these niggas disloyal! She knew the only person she could trust in the game was herself. She called Tasha to let her know what had just happened.

"Girl, this nigga just tried to have me killed!"

"What?! Who?!"

"That fat-ass pig Block."

"Bitch, I'ma kill that nigga! What happened?"

"This nigga sent his shooter. Some young nigga named LA."

"You talking about Little LA?"

"Girl, I don't know. That nigga could've killed me right there though."

"Why didn't he? What happened?"

"He told me he wants to work for me. Says he can't really trust Block's ass anymore. He been acting too erratic and havin' shit go sideways."

"Bitch, that little-ass nigga is a shooter, for real. You need to call him."

"I know."

"You okay?"

"Yeah. He scared the hell out of me at first."

"You want to come over here?"

"Yeah, Girl! Let me call this nigga first though."

"Alright, let me know when you're headed this way."

Block started to worry when he didn't hear from LA. His mind was racing as he thought where the little nigga could be. Block had a personal relationship with Omar, Roc's brother. He knew that Omar didn't fuck with that bitch either, so it would be easy to get info on her from "Doggie Bone." He called him up.

"Omar, what up doe?"

"Who the fuck is this?"

"It's Block, Nigga."

"How the fuck you get my number?"

"You know these hoes be talking."

"Yeah? So what's up?"

"Shit. I wanted to talk some business with you."

"Well, talk, Nigga."

"You know I heard your brother got shot."

"That shit ain't your business."

"No disrespect. I'm just letting you know what happened after that."

"Talk, Nigga. What happened?"

"Your brother's bitch called me trying to sell me some dope."

"What?!"

"Yeah, that's what I said. She say she got ten keys."

"What?! That bitch ain't got ten keys of shit."

"Well, she pulled up on me with a zip of 'dog.'"

"Oh yeah?"

"Yeah, and I just thought you'd like to know."

"Good looking. Look though, I'ma hit you back when I find out what the deal is."

"Alright. Just hit me up, you know, with a finder's fee or something." He laughed to try to make light of it, but they both knew he was serious.

"Yeah. I got you," Omar replied dryly before hanging up on any further conversation. Then, he started thinking about where the fuck that bitch could have gotten ten keys from. He didn't know, but he was damn sure gonna find out.

"Girl, c'mon! We gonna miss this nigga Pooh!" Tasha yelled to Sydney. It was time for their meeting.

"Bitch, I had to get the dope."

"Did you call Little LA?"

"Shit, I was packing so fast, I forgot. I'm about to now. But I thought you knew this Pooh."

"I do. That don't mean I trust his ass."

"Alright, let me call LA."

The phone rang several times before there was an answer.

When he did pick up, Sydney could hear "Don't Know" from Luca Brasi 3 playing in the background.

"Who this?!"

"Sydney."

"Oh yeah. What up doe?"

"Look, you still want that job?"

"Yeah. What you need?"

"I got to drop something off, and I need somebody to watch my back."

"Okay. Say less. I'ma meet you on 7 Mile and Mansfield at the Fat Burgers."

"Okay. I'll be there in five minutes." Sydney hung up and headed out the door.

"Where you at?" LA asked Sydney on the phone after pulling up to Fat Burgers and not seeing her.

"We're parked in the black Range Rover. Is that you in the Hellcat?"

"Yeah, this me." He pulled up next to Sydney and rolled his window down. "So, who we meeting?"

"This nigga. I just need you to watch me and my girl's back."

"I got you. Don't worry about shit."

"Yeah, alright." Sydney smiled, but neither of them knew that Omar had followed Sydney and was right behind her - watching everything.

"What the fuck she meeting up with this little nigga for?" Omar wondered as he watched and waited.

Omar thought that Block was trying to get him hit because he knew that LA was Block's shooter. So, he decided to call Block up and find out just what in the fuck was going on.

When Block answered, Omar could hear Moneybagg Yo and Lil Baby's "FWM" playing, but he didn't care about the nigga's vibe and cut straight into him.

"Nigga, who the fuck you think you're fucking with?!"

"Hold on, Bruh," Block said, while pushing his girl off of him.

"Damn, Nigga! You ain't have to push me!" Block's girl CC yelled.

"Bitch, shut the fuck up. Now back to you, Nigga. Who the fuck is this calling me with all this animosity in your voice?!"

"Nigga, stop acting like you don't know who the fuck this is."

Block looked down at the phone. "Omar?"

"Yeah, Nigga."

"Damn, Bruh. What's the problem?"

"That little nigga LA, that's the problem."

"My Nigga, I'm lost. I ain't talked to that nigga in days."

"Then why the fuck is he following that bitch around like he her bodyguard?"

"What?! Look, Omar, I don't know what the fuck you're talking about. I'm gonna find out though."

"Yeah, you do that."

Omar continued to watch as Sydney met up with Pooh next.

"Damn, I almost left," Pooh said. "I hope this hit is worth the wait."

"I'm sorry we were late," Tasha said, smiling at Pooh and walking towards him with her arms open.

He was surprised to see two of the baddest girls in the city walking in looking like super models.

Sydney was high-yellow and thick as hell with hair all the way down her back.

Tasha was just as thick and as chocolate as he remembered her being ... yeah, mouth-watering chocolate.

"This my girl Sydney," Tasha said.

"So, you're the plug, huh?" Pooh asked Sydney.

"Look, I'm here to talk business, so plug or no plug, I'm the bitch with the dope," Sydney said seriously.

Pooh smiled. "Okay, Boss Lady. Let's get down to business. I need three keys."

"That's it?" Sydney asked.

"Hold on, Queen. That's just for now. If it's pure like your girl said you got, we're gonna definitely do more business. So, what's the ticket?"

"Forty-five a key."

"Okay. You got a test for me?"

"Sure do. LA, bring the man his test."

LA walked over to Pooh with a chip bag in his hand. "Here you go."

"Good lookin'. Damn, don't I know you from somewhere?"

"Naw, My Nigga."

"I guess you just got one of those faces."

"Yeah, guess so." LA looked around at the nearly empty venue then exited the building.

"Back to business. Okay, Queen, let me take this to my tester. When I know something, I'ma call."

"Alright, I hope to hear from you soon," Sydney said.

"Tasha, it's been fun." Pooh got up from the table and reached across it to shake Syndey's hand. "Okay, Queen. We're gonna talk." As Pooh walked out of the building, Sydney texted LA that she and Tasha were on their way out. LA called her back immediately and told her to hold up.

"What's up?" Sydney asked.

"This fat nigga Block talking crazy."

"What he say?"

"Hold on. I'm just gonna send you the text."

Sydney sat stunned as she read Block's text. It read: *"Look, you disloyal muthafucka, you thought you could hide that shit from me? You and that bitch dead. I hope the pussy worth your life!"*

"That fat piece of shit!" Sydney said.

"Look, Boss Lady, I work for you now. So, I'll move how you say move, but this nigga a problem. We need to get him out of the way."

"No. I'm not doing that."

"Sometimes, it ain't your choice. This the dope game. Ain't no free passes in this shit." LA was hoping he was convincing, but Sydney was adamant.

"No. I won't have that shit on my conscience," she

finally responded.

Omar kept watching. He knew he had to pick his moment.

He had driven by his brother's house last night. He didn't see Sydney, but he did see the police driving by slowly. They must be keeping an eye on the place. He'd have to strike when they all least expected it.

CHAPTER 5

Later, Tasha was pulling up to her girl CC's house, when she saw her washing a S550 that looked like Block's.

"Bitch, whose car is that?" Tasha asked.

"Girl, it's this new nigga I'm fucking with, shit. Why?"

"You talking to that fat-ass pig Block?"

"Yeah. How you know him?"

"Bitch, that's Syd's ex."

"What?"

"Yeah, and that nigga just tried to have Syd killed!"

"Bitch, you're lying! I'm done with that nigga!"

"Naw. Stay with the nigga so we can know what the fuck he on."

"Girl, I ain't trying to be in the mix with all this shit."

"Bitch, we need you to stay with that nigga. Look, I gotta go now, but we need you to pull through with this nigga, for real."

"Alright."

"Good. I'm out, but call me later. Love you."

"I love you too, and I got you. Bye."

Meanwhile, Pooh was in the trap with his uncle. "Aye, Unk, I got one for you. I need you to test this out for me."

"C'mon, Nephew, let's see what you got here."

He reached into his bag and pulled out his works. He tied his belt around his arm, making the veins bulge. He put the little pack of tan powder into the bent, burnt spoon.

He eyed the powder closely as he added a couple of drops of water to the spoon and held the lighter under it.

After it had dissolved and he'd put the cotton ball in it, Unk pulled the liquid heroin into the needle and shot it into his arm.

"Ooowee, Nephew. That shit Grade A. Damn!"

"What can it take?"

"At least a six or seven."

"Oh yeah?" Pooh grabbed his phone from the table and called Tasha. "Tasha?"

"What up doe, Pooh? I take it you like that shit, uh?"

"That shit was Grade A. Tell your girl I need six, tomorrow."

"Say less. Same spot, tomorrow at five."

"Fa' sho', Queen."

Tasha was so happy, she screamed with excitement.

She knew Sydney was on her way to the hospital

to visit Roc, but she hoped she could catch her before she got there.

"Hello?"

"Girl, you're not gonna believe who just called."

"Bitch, I don't have time for the *Guess Who* game. So, who was it?"

"Girl, that nigga Pooh."

"What he say?"

"He wants to meet up tomorrow to pick up six."

Sydney started smiling, thinking that her nightmare was almost over. "Girl! Hell yeah! Look, I'm about to walk into the hospital to see Roc, so I'll call you back."

"You better than me; 'cause even after that nigga put you in all this shit, you still loyal."

Sydney remained silent for a minute, taking in what Tasha was saying because she knew she was right. They talked a bit longer before hanging up.

She was loyal to a fault. She was so busy thinking about what Tasha had said, she didn't notice Omar following her to the hospital.

She walked into the lobby and up to the receptionist's desk. "Hi, I'm here to see Rockail Williams."

"Okay. Your name?"

"Sydney Williams."

"Mrs. Williams, you do know that visiting hours are over at 9 o'clock?"

"Yes, I'm aware."

"Okay then. Here's your visitor's pass."

"Thank you." Sydney was still so unaware of her

surroundings, that she didn't see Omar coming in behind her as she was getting onto the elevator. As the doors were closing, Omar was walking up to the receptionist's desk.

"Aye," he said. "I need Rockail's room number."

"Excuse me, Sir. Are you on the visitor's list?"

"I'm his fucking brother."

"Sorry, Sir. We don't have you on the list."

"Bitch, fuck that list! What's the fucking number?" Omar didn't wait for her to answer. Instead, he reached +out and grabbed her computer screen and turned it so he could look for Roc's number for himself.

"Sir! You can't do that! Security!!!" The receptionist yelled to get the security guard's attention. The security rushed over to help as she attempted to turn the screen back around. "Sir, let the screen go!"

The guard grabbed Omar's arms, trying to get him under control, but Omar turned around and swung on the guard, knocking him out. "Bitch, I said what's the fucking room number?!"

The receptionist was crying and screaming out the room number. "2121! He's in room 2121! Please, don't hurt me!"

Omar rushed to the elevators to go up to the room to catch Sydney, who had no idea what was going on in the lobby – or what was coming her way.

She made it to Roc's room, nervous to see her husband's condition today. She could never get used to it. She slowly walked in and looked around the corner.

When she saw Roc hooked up to the heart monitor, the emotions flooded back, and she broke down and began crying.

"Roc! Baby! I was so mad at you for leaving me with all this shit to deal with. But now, all I want is for you to get better."

The room door suddenly swung open. Sydney looked up in shock to see her brother-in-law coming to stand over her.

"Omar!"

"Bitch, you thought I wasn't going to find out?!" He grabbed her, pulling her away from Roc's bed. He grabbed her around the neck and pushed her against the wall.

"Omar, I didn't say nothing!"

"Bitch, I'm not talking about the police! I'm talking about the keys you around here flexing!"

"Look, Omar, I don't know what kind of information you been getting, but whoever telling you that shit is wrong."

"Stop fucking lying! Where the fuck is the dope at?!"

"I don't have any dope!"

"Bitch, you think I'm playing with you?" Omar yelled as he began choking her.

Sydney was crying and trying to push Omar off her. "Please, Omar! Please!"

As Sydney started to lose consciousness, four security guards rushed in and pulled Omar off of her.

Omar broke free of the guards' grips and took off towards the fire exit. The guards regained their balance, and two took off after Omar.

"Ma'am, are you okay?"

"Yeah."

"The police are on the way."

"I'm okay."

"Ma'am, you should let the doctors take a look at you."

Sydney started looking around for her purse so she could call LA. She went to a quiet corner and dialed him. When he answered, she could hear people laughing.

"Hello."

"So while niggas out here trying to kill me, you partying and shit?!" Sydney whispered harshly into the phone.

"Wait. What's going on?"

"I'll explain when you get here. I'm at Receiving Hospital. Hurry up."

"I'll be there in ten minutes."

Sydney knew she was safe at the hospital right now until LA got there, so she sat back by Roc's bed and waited for LA's arrival.

CHAPTER 6

LA pulled up to the hospital, following the police cars. All he could do was keep telling himself he didn't know what the fuck was going on, but he thought it best that he put his strap up. When he walked into the hospital, he immediately saw Sydney standing in the lobby with two security guards and a police officer.

Sydney looked up and saw LA standing by the door. She started yelling at the guards, "Look, I told y'all I don't know that nigga! I don't know what's going on."

"Ma'am, you have to give us something. The receptionist stated the perpetrator claimed to be your husband's brother."

"I never seen that nigga before. I don't have shit to give y'all. So, can I go?"

"We can't, in good faith, let you drive home by yourself."

"I'm not. My friend is over there. He came to pick me up."

"Okay," the officer replied. He then walked over to LA. "Excuse me, Sir. Are you here to pick up this lady?"

"Yeah. Sydney, what's going on?"

"I don't know. I just want to get out of here."

LA wrapped his arm around Sydney's shoulder as they walked out of the hospital together. The whole time, Sydney was mumbling, "How the fuck did that nigga know about the keys?"

"I told you that nigga was gonna be a problem." LA slammed the car door in frustration after she had gotten in.

"It wasn't Block," Sydney said after LA got in on his side.

"What? Then who the fuck was it?"

"Omar."

"Omar? Ain't that nigga your brother-in-law? Why the fuck would he want to kill you?"

"Because, he's the one who put my husband in his coma in the first place." Sydney started crying, thinking about all of the shit she'd been through recently.

"Look, Queen, for me to be able to protect you, I need to know everything."

So, Sydney told him everything. From Omar shooting Roc, to the two million dollars that he had taken, to how she now owed the plug Roc's debt and how the plug had given her a chance to work the debt off.

When Sydney finished, she let out a deep breath, relieved just to be able to get some of the weight off of her shoulders.

"Damn, Boss Lady, that shit sounds crazy. So, what's the next move?"

"I don't know." LA was pulling up in front of Sydney's house. "But look, can you stay here at the house tonight?" she asked him. She didn't want to go back to Tasha's and take a chance of leading someone to her home. Tasha was doing enough for her and the boys.

LA could see the fear on her face when he looked at her. "Okay, I got you, Boss Lady. With the police involved, these niggas might be too spooked to show themselves right now, but you can't count on that shit."

"Thanks," Sydney said with a sense of relief, knowing she would be safe – at least for the night.

When LA walked in, he took a good look at the house this time.

"You can get the boys' room." Sydney walked into the other room to grab some clothes for him.

"I don't know if these will fit you," she said, handing him the clothes. "You good?"

"Yeah, I'm good."

"If you need to take a shower, the bathroom is right across the hall."

"Alright."

Sydney went to her room and started taking off her clothes so she could take a shower herself.

As she was wrapping her hair up, she thought about what LA had asked her, and even though she didn't know exactly what her next move would be, she knew she couldn't let niggas take shit from her. And if she had to, she would do whatever it took to keep her family safe.

She was so deep in thought after her shower that she forgot LA was there and walked out of the bathroom completely naked - just as LA was coming back from the kitchen.

Sydney jumped in surprise and said, "Damn, I forgot you were here!"

LA was stunned to see Sydney standing in the hallway naked, still damp from her shower. He couldn't believe how gorgeous she was. "Damn, Ma."

"Nigga, act like you seen pussy before!" Sydney said with a smirk on her face. She knew LA wanted her, but she could never let a nigga play her - especially not now. She had no room for love or mistakes. She was focused on her boys and her money.

Later the next day, LA awoke to the smell of pancakes. "Okay, Boss Lady," he said, walking into the kitchen. "You on your domesticated shit," he smiled.

"Why I gotta be domesticated to do something nice?" Sydney started laughing.

"I'm just joking. But on some real shit though, we gotta come up with a plan, 'cause from what I know about both of those niggas, that shit ain't gonna rest easy."

"Yeah, I know." Before she could go any further, she heard her phone ringing in the other room. She left LA to eat his late brunch. "Hello?"

"Girl, is you gonna be ready to go meet that nigga Pooh?" Tasha asked.

"Yeah, I'll be on time. Hold on, somebody calling on my other line." Sydney switched over. "Hello?"

"Mom, we tired of staying over here with this mean old lady," Rocko said. He was mad at Sydney because he hadn't seen her or his father in so long.

"I'm coming to get y'all tomorrow. I promise." Sydney said the words, but she didn't know if it was the truth or not.

She did know it wasn't safe to bring the boys home just yet. "In the meantime, y'all better be good over Mrs. Jackson's house though."

"Okay, Mama," Rocko said. Then, Sydney could hear Rocky in the background yelling to speak to her. "Alright! Dang, Dude! Stop yelling," Rocko said.

"Hello?" Rocky said. "Ma, when you coming to get us?"

"Tomorrow, Rocky."

"For real, Ma?"

"Yeah, for real, Baby. Look, I gotta go. I'ma call you later. I love you."

"Okay, Ma, love you too."

Sydney clicked back over to Tasha.

"Girl, who the fuck you have me on hold so long for?"

"My boys."

While she was talking, LA walked into the room. "Aye, I'm about to jump in the shower. You got some clean towels?"

"Yeah, they're in the hallway closet."

"Girl," Tasha interrupted, "who the fuck was that?"

"That was LA."

"What? You got that little nigga taking showers at your house?"

"Girl, it ain't like that. He just stayed the night."

"Oh. So you fucking that nigga?"

Sydney laughed. "Bitch, I'm about to come over there. Stop playing."

"Uh huh. I'll see you when you get here," Tasha said and hung up.

After coming out of the shower later, LA said, "You need a team."

"What? I don't know nobody in this life. The people I thought I could trust are the ones that's been trying to kill me."

"Let me put together your team so you can focus on your family and not all of the bullshit that comes with this life."

"Why do you want to help me? You don't know me or owe me shit, so why help?"

"Why help? You're a survivor, and in the dope game, loyalty is the only way you survive."

The way he said it, Sydney knew in her heart that she could trust LA. "So, I can trust you? Alright, grab that bag out of the closet."

CHAPTER 7

Sydney and LA jumped in the car and pulled off. They were listening to Lil Baby's "Errbody" when Sydney told LA they had to swing by Tasha's apartment to pick her up.

"You need to make a decision about Doggy Bone, Sydney," LA said, worried about her safety.

"I know. I'ma figure it out."

"That bitch think I'm playing with her," Omar mumbled to himself in the car. "But, I'ma kill that bitch." Omar slid over to Sydney's house to finish the job.

He'd had to lay low last night after leaving the hospital, just in case people were looking for him.

When he pulled up, he noticed that her car wasn't there and figured she may have left it at the hospital.

He jumped out with his gun in his hand and walked onto the porch. He peeked through the window but didn't see anybody, so he went around to the back. He kicked the door open and went in.

"Bitch, where the fuck you at?!" he yelled.

He searched the house, looking for Sydney and her boys. When he didn't find either, he knew something was up, so he called Block.

"What up doe?" Block answered.

"Not a muthafucking thing. I'm at this bitch Sydney's house, but she ain't here and neither is those little niggas of hers."

"Yeah?" Block stopped and said to his woman CC, "Hold on, Baby. I'm on the phone." Then back to Omar, "So, what's the move?"

"I'ma stay here until she shows up."

"Let me make some calls to the streets and find her," Block said.

CC interrupted the conversation. "Damn, nigga! See that's what I'm talking about!" she yelled at Block.

"Bitch, I got shit to do! Let yourself out," Block told her while getting out of bed and walking towards the door.

CC looked at him with a confused look on her face. "Who the fuck you think you're talking to?"

Block slammed the bedroom door behind him, but CC heard him call the person Omar in the hall. She threw the clock from the nightstand at him. "Fat-ass nigga!" she yelled, then pulled out her phone and called Tasha.

"Hello?" Tasha answered.

"Girl, I'm at that nigga Block's right now, and I just heard him talking to some nigga named Omar. Well, that nigga was talking loud as hell, and I heard him say he at Sydney house right now."

"What? He said he's there right now?"

"Yeah," CC whispered. "That's what he said."

"You're fa' sho' that's what you heard?"

"Yeah, Bitch. I know what I heard."

"Alright. Let me hit you back." Tasha was nervous as she dialed Sydney's number because she knew that Sydney had been at the house the last time they had talked. When Sydney didn't answer, Tasha began to really worry. She hung up and called right back but still got no answer.

As soon as she slammed the phone down in frustration, it began to ring. She didn't even look to see who was calling, she just snatched it up.

"Hello?! Sydney?!"

"Yeah. Why the fuck is you blowing me up? I told you we was on our way."

"Bitch, Omar at your house!"

"What?! How you know that?"

"You remember Ciara?"

"CC from the club?"

"Yeah. She fucking that nigga Block."

"What? Are you serious?"

"I told her to stay with the nigga so we would know what the fuck he up to, and now we know. She just heard him talking to Omar."

"So, that's where that nigga getting his information from." Sydney looked at LA, who was watching intently. "Look, we just pulled up, Tasha. Come out."

"Here I come." Tasha rushed outside and looked around the parking lot for Sydney's truck but didn't see it.

"Tasha! Tasha!" Sydney yelled out of the window of LA's car. Tasha heard Sydney, ran over, and hopped in the back seat.

"Girl, where your truck at?"

"At the hospital."

"What? Why you leave it there, and how you end up with this little nigga chauffeuring you around?"

"It's a long story, and I'll tell you later. Right now, let's focus on this deal with Pooh. Did you call that nigga?"

"I was waiting on y'all to get here, but I'ma call him right now." Tasha dialed the number and heard a few rings before Pooh answered.

"What up doe?"

"Shit. Me and my girl ready to pull up."

"Say less. You can meet me at my people house on Six Mile and Mansfield." He described the house to her.

"Alright, we'll be there in like twenty-five minutes."

"I'll be right out front."

Before they pulled off, LA told Sydney to open up the glove box. When she did, she was shocked to see a gun. "What's this for?"

"It's for you. Just in case shit don't go right." Sydney looked stunned. She couldn't even remember the last time she actually held a gun. Then, she flashed back to the first time she met Roc outside her parents' house.

Sydney had grown up there under very strict rules, so as a teenager, she rebelled and always went for the bad boys. The day she met Roc, she was home alone when she heard a loud commotion outside. When she opened the door, she saw a young, skinny, short kid with a black Cutlass arguing with her neighbor, Mr. Jenkins.

"Look here, Young Nigga," Mr. Jenkins was yelling, "I'ma pay you on the first."

"Muthafucka, I told you don't have me come out here for nothing."

Mr. Jenkins pulled out a Glock and stared right at the young guy. "Now what, Little Nigga?"

Roc swung at Mr. Jenkins, knocking him down and falling on top of him in the process. The gun fell from Mr. Jenkins' hand, and they were both fighting - struggling to reach the gun that had fallen right by Sydney's foot. She had unconsciously run over there. She didn't know why, but she reached down and grabbed the gun.

"Get the fuck off of him, Mr. Jenkins!" she yelled.

"You little bitch. What you gonna do with that gun? Man, give me that shit!" he screamed at her.

"Get your ol' ass outta here!" Sydney yelled.

"Okay, Little Muthafucka. I'ma remember this shit."

Mr. Jenkins got up and sulked off.

"Thanks, Little Ma," Roc said.

"You're welcome, but why that old ass nigga pull his strap on you?"

"He's a dope fiend, that's why."

"Oh, you're a dope boy."

"Hold up, Little Ma. I ain't no dope boy. I'm a

business man."

"Yeah, okay," she said, holding back her smile.

"My name's Roc. Can I get yours? I mean … since you saved my life and all, I think it's only right we at least know each other's name."

"It's Sydney, but people call me Syd."

When they pulled up to the house on Six Mile and Mansfield, Sydney snapped back to reality and left the past in her daydreams. "Is that him?" Sydney asked Tasha, referring to the house.

"I don't know. Let me call him right quick."

"Hello?"

"What's up, Pooh? We here. Where you at?"

"That's y'all in the Hellcat?"

"Yeah."

Pooh opened the front door and waved at them. "Come on in," he said.

"You stay behind with the bag," Sydney told LA. "Just in case…."

LA was worried, but he knew he had to trust her decision. "Okay," he said. "But take this though." He reached down and took one of the guns from his waistband. He handed it to Tasha so she'd also have some protection.

"Okay," Sydney said, taking a deep breath. "Let's go make this money."

The two women got out of the car and walked to the trunk. Sydney reached into the duffle bag and pulled out one key. She put the key in her purse, and they walked onto the porch and through the door that Pooh had left open. When they walked in, the first thing they saw was that there were other people in the house.

"Damn, Ma. You thick as hell," Pooh's little homie Ty said to Sydney.

"Look here, Little Nigga, we ain't here for all that!" she clapped back.

Pooh and his homies started laughing. Ty's pride got the best of him, and he jumped up in Sydney's face.

"Bitch, who the fuck do you think you're talking to?!"

Sydney and Tasha both pulled out the guns that LA had given them.

"You, Nigga!" Sydney yelled, pointing her gun right at Ty's face. "Now, sit the fuck down. Damn, Pooh, is this how you do business?"

"Naw, Queens. Put the guns down. All is well. My little niggas just be acting crazy sometimes, but that's on me. Now, let's get down to business."

"Yeah, alright." They followed him into a back room where there were females counting stacks of hundred-dollar bills.

"Now, for the business. I need six keys at that same number."

Sydney reached into her bag and handed him the key she had.

"Hold up," Pooh said with a confused look on his face. "Where the fuck is the rest of my dope?"

"Don't panic," Sydney said, reaching back into her bag and pulling out her phone. She quickly dialed

LA's number. "Yeah. Everything's good. Bring five."

LA grabbed five more keys from the trunk, went up to the porch and knocked on the door.

"Nigga, who is you?" Ty asked him.

"I'm with Syd."

"Nigga, I don't give a fuck who you with. Why is you here?"

Pooh could hear Ty in the front room arguing with somebody and came out. "Let that nigga in," he said.

LA walked past Ty, who was mean-mugging him. Ty was thinking to himself that he knew LA from somewhere.

"The man of the hour," Pooh said. "Let's get to it."

Pooh looked over at one of the females counting the money. "Aye, Lil Ma, count out two seventy for the boss lady." The two females picked up stacks of hundreds and started counting out the money.

After a few minutes had gone by, the girls handed LA two hundred and seventy thousand dollars. "There you go, Boss Lady," Pooh said. "I'ma need the same thing next month."

Sydney was relieved that everything had gone right. She was two hundred and seventy thousand dollars closer to getting outta the dope game.

When they were walking out the house, Ty remembered where he knew LA from.

"That's the little nigga that killed Flip!" he whispered fiercely to Pooh.

"What?" Pooh asked, confused.

"Bro, that's the nigga!"

"Little Nigga, chill out 'cause you about to fuck up my money," Pooh said. Ty got quiet, but he wasn't happy about it.

Sydney couldn't wait to call Goddess with the good news. "Hello? Ms. Golden? It's me – Sydney. Can we meet up?"

"Call me Goddess."

"Okay, Goddess."

"Sure, we can meet. When?"

"In a couple of hours, if you're available."

"That's fine. Come to my house. Let me give you the address."

"Okay," Sydney replied. She listened and then hung up.

"Before we go anywhere," LA said, "we need to drop some money and this work off."

"Yeah, I know." Sydney knew she couldn't take it back to the house, not with Omar still out there looking for her. She was trying to think of a safe place when she remembered the storage unit she and Roc had gotten back in the day.

"Aye, shoot to Safe Lockers storage units," she told LA and gave him the address. Sydney repeated Ms. Golden's address a few more times in her head to lock it in as they rode down the street.

CHAPTER 8

LA, Sydney and Tasha pulled up to Safe Lockers.

"Pull around to the back," Sydney told LA. "It's the second from the last." She remembered the combination to the lock was her birthday. She entered 9-3-89 into the lock, and it popped open. She lifted the rolling door up and stepped into the unit. She started moving boxes around, noticed her wedding dress, and flashed back to the night before her wedding.

"I can't believe we're getting married tomorrow and I'm going to be Mrs. Williams," Sydney said, smiling in excitement over the upcoming big day. They were staying at the Motor City Hotel for the wedding.

Roc was anxious as well. Sydney saw that he looked worried, so she handed him her purse and undid his tie.

"You know I love you, right?" Her comment caught him off guard. She brushed a few stray hairs off of his suit and took her bag back. He pressed up against her with his lips to her ear and repeated, "You know I love you, right? More than anything."

"Whatever, Nigga. Don't even front. Ain't shit changed. Same shit, different day," she mumbled

teasingly as she tried to lean away but couldn't.

He lightly kissed her ear, her cheek, and moved down to her neck. Roc wouldn't let her go completely. He turned her, and they began to walk slowly to the desk as if they were glued together. With each step, Sydney could feel his dick pressing up against her ass.

"Okay, you can let me go now," Sydney told him.

"Whatever, Nigga," he mocked her.

"Oh, you got jokes now? Roc, don't do this to me. We're not fucking. Remember, 'After the wedding?'"

"I'm sorry, Baby." He was licking her neck, easing his hand down her skirt. "I love you … I want you," he whispered and gently rubbed her clit, causing her to move sensually.

He began planting firm but tender kisses on her neck. Sydney let out a low moan. Now, his lips had her feeling hot. She was getting caught up in the moment, melting in his arms.

"I love you, Syd," he mumbled again as he began unbuttoning her blouse. His scent overtook her. It seemed like the entire room smelled just like him.

Her knees got weak, and that meant that it was time for her to go. She wiggled out of his arms when she heard him reach back to lock the door.

"I told you - after the wedding. Why are you locking the door?" she snapped.

"I want to talk."

"Whatever, Nigga. I bet you do." She laughed, and Roc knew he was busted as he watched her turn and hurry towards the door.

"Hold up." He grabbed her around the waist with her

back to his chest. He picked up where he left off. She gave up and tossed her purse towards the sofa, barely missing. He opened her blouse, and this time, she didn't resist. He eased her bra past her nipples and began playing with them, rolling them between his thumbs and middle fingers – just the way she liked it. Hearing the way she was moaning let him know he was on point and brought a sly grin to his face.

He mumbled in her ear while sliding her legs apart and rubbing her pussy through her wet panties.

"Baby," she moaned as she wiggled her ass against his hard dick. He slipped two fingers into her panties and began massaging her clit. The shit he was doing made her pussy so wet, her entire body began to jerk. The harder he pressed her clit, the louder she squealed, telling him how good it felt.

"Does this pussy want Daddy?" he breathed in her ear as she was on the verge of cumming. She couldn't speak. "Whose is it?" he pressed.

"It's … uh … all yours, Daddy," she grunted. "Y-yes!" Her juices squirted all over his hand.

While she caught her breath, Roc took the opportunity to ease her blouse all the way off and toss it onto the couch.

He pushed a stack of papers over on the desk, picked her up and sat her on top of the desk. He slid her panties off and unzipped his fly. She slid his pants and boxers down while he unsnapped her bra. Before he could get the straps over her shoulders, he was sucking and biting her nipples.

"Mmmmmm," she moaned as she gently pushed him

back and reached down, squeezing and massaging his throbbing dick with both hands. She slid closer to the edge of the desk and roughly grabbed his ass.

"Damn, Baby!" he grunted. "That's the shit I'm talking 'bout. Shhhh-it!"

"This is my dick," Sydney said, squeezing it harder. It was her turn to take control.

"This dick …. ssss … fuck, Baby … just like that."

"It's Mommy's - right, Daddy?"

"D-damn right," he stuttered as she gently massaged his nuts.

"Nigga, act like it." She released her grip, leaned back and propped one of her stilettos up on the desk. She pulled his dick to her pussy and began rubbing the head up and down her hot, juicy pussy, teasing them both. Roc was enjoying the view of seeing his dick being handled between her small, French-manicured fingers.

"Okay, okay. This feels soooo damn good. Oh …. yes!" she screamed as her body spazzed. She kept the dick on her clit, riding her orgasm higher and higher.

There was a knock at the door. "Girl, come on! We ready to go." It was Tasha, Sydney's best friend, along with her bridesmaids. They were supposed to be going out for a bridal party.

"Fuck!" Roc spat.

"Oh shit!" Sydney gasped and shook as she tried to catch her breath. She had a smirk on her face as she gently pushed Roc back and slid down off the desk.

He was standing there with his rock-hard dick in his hand. She clumsily fastened her bra and snatched her blouse from the couch.

She wobbled over to the door, her knees still weak from the two toe-curling, much-needed orgasms.

He grabbed her hands, pulling her close and massaging her ass. She was still trying to get out of the room to celebrate as he covered her mouth with his, kissing her deep and long.

Coming up for air, he whispered, "Let's finish where we left off."

"You want some of this fat, juicy, pregnant pussy, don't you?" she teased.

"Baby, you know there's nothing I want more right now."

"You're going to keep on wanting it too. After the wedding." She pushed him away.

"Syd."

"Syd, nothing."

"So you're just gonna let a nigga get blue balls?"

She laughed. "I know you're horny. Shit, I'm horny too, but we made a promise not to have sex the night before the wedding. Now, the girls are here, and I gotta go."

"I know, Baby, but ..."

"Hold that thought for me. It'll be worth it, Daddy." She broke free, grabbed her panties and the rest of her belongings, and headed for the door.

"Syd! Syd!"

"Yeah?"

"Girl, where the fuck did you just go?" Tasha asked, back in the present in the storage unit.

"I was thinking about Roc, looking at this damn

wedding dress."

"Bitch, you better get your mind together. Fuck that nigga. I know you love him, but his shit got niggas trying to kill you and your boys."

Sydney and their girl CC had filled Tasha in on everything that she'd missed over the last twenty-four hours.

"I know." Sydney went back to the car and grabbed the duffle bag out of the trunk. She, LA and Tasha started counting the money. She took a hundred and eighty thousand off for the plug. She gave Tasha ten thousand and LA ten thousand.

CHAPTER 9

LA looked over at Tasha, confused about the money. They both turned back to Sydney.

"Bitch, you don't owe me shit. You my sister, period," Tasha said to Sydney, rolling her neck. Sydney smiled, knowing her best friend was in her corner. She and Tasha had been friends since middle school, and even then, Tasha was her "Ride or Die."

LA was still looking confused when he reached out to give Sydney back the ten stacks. She was shocked that he was giving her back the money. She wasn't used to people doing for her. Shakily, she reached out for the money.

"Look, Ma, when you get back on your feet then hit my hand," LA said.

Sydney nodded her head at LA.

She started thinking about paying the plug back as she was putting the money back into the bag.

She looked up at LA and rattled off an address. "That's the address we need to head to now."

LA looked at her and said, "You know this shit across Eight Mile, right?"

Sydney looked back at Tasha, who was stashing the keys of dope in the back of the locker. "Yeah, I know."

"Shit, it's okay with me, Boss Lady, as long as you know shit hot across Eight Mile," LA replied.

Sydney, LA and Tasha jumped back into the car and headed on the way to Ms. Golden's house. Sliding up Eight Mile, they started seeing more and more police cars the closer they got to Woodward Avenue. *A simple drop off*, Sydney thought ... *we good.*

"Shit hot," LA said, looking around nervously. "Oh shit! Damn, I just ran a red light. Hopefully, the hook didn't see us," LA said, looking frustratedly over at Sydney.

"Oh shit! They flicking the lights. Fuck! I can't be going to jail. I'm too cute for that shit," Tasha mumbled, panicking about the police.

"Calm down. We straight. It's just a traffic stop. Don't panic," Sydney said, looking back at Tasha in the back seat. She wanted to believe it. She knew if the police searched the car, it was no way she could explain the two seventy in the trunk.

"Man, fuck this shit." LA reached in his stash spot and pulled his Glock out.

"Nigga, what the fuck is you doing?" Sydney yelled at LA.

"Whatchu mean? We got two seventy in the trunk of the car."

Sydney looked around for a place for them to pull over. "Just chill out and pull over there." It was still light outside. She wanted to find a place out of the view of the public eye. "Put that gun up!" Sydney said to LA, but it was too late to put it back in the stash spot, because before they could come to a complete stop, the officer was already getting out of the squad car.

Tasha and Sydney looked back at the officer. To their disappointment, it was a tall White man with a rugged beard. As he walked closer to the car, LA rushed to stash his gun under his t-shirt.

Tap, tap.

"How you doing, Officer …" LA paused, looking for the officer's badge, "… Night."

"Well, Boy, I'll be better after I have your license and registration in my hand," Night said in a southern accent.

"Okay, Officer, let me get the registration out of the glove box." LA reached over to Sydney to grab the registration, and the barrel of the Glock showed from under his t-shirt.

Night saw the barrel of the gun. "Put 'cha fucking hands up, you son of a bitch!"

"Okay, okay! Fuck!" LA yelled, throwing his hands on the steering wheel.

Sydney just shook her head, putting her hands on the dashboard in disbelief of what had just happened. She started mumbling to herself, "Damn, what the fuck am I going to tell Ms. Golden?"

Night was calling for backup when he heard the passenger say the name *Golden.*

"Whatchu say?" the officer yelled at Sydney with an alarmed look on his face.

Sydney had already said too much. "I ain't say nothing."

The officer became nervous when he heard Golden's name. "Did you say *Golden*?!" Night was yelling as his radio was going off.

Sydney looked over at him with her hands up on the dashboard. She saw fear in his face but not from them. *Just the thought that I had said Golden's name sent fear down his spine.*

Sydney thought about it for a moment more and decided to tell Night who she was. "My name's Sydney, and I work for … Golden."

Night's radio went off, and he grabbed it.

"Officer Night, is everything alright?" the dispatch officer asked.

"Just a traffic stop."

"Do you need any backup, Night?"

Night looked down at Sydney and responded to the dispatcher, "Everything's good." He disengaged from his radio then turned to Sydney and said, "Wait here."

"Okay," Sydney said. She looked around, confused and scared.

The officer walked away from the car, pulling out his phone. Sydney looked back at Officer Night. She couldn't make out what he was saying, but she knew it must've been important because he looked like he was on the phone with his boss.

Night walked back up to the car. "Sorry for that. Here goes your license and registration. Sydney, right? Ms. Golden said next time to call her and inform her you are on the way. Have a nice day."

That was the first time Sydney saw how much

power the older lady really had. LA looked at Sydney with a *Who the fuck you got us working for* look on his face. When they pulled off, nobody said anything. They couldn't believe what had just happened.

"Aye, is this the house?" Sydney asked.

"Yeah, it's the address in the GPS," LA responded.

"Damn, this like some ol' rich White people shit right here," Tasha said as they pulled into the gated house with guards everywhere.

That's when shit started to get real for them. This wasn't no corner-boy operation. The driveway to this house was as long as the blocks they grew up on. It was filled with white Rolls-Royces and a G-Wagon Benz.

Once they pulled up to the front door, one of the bodyguards with two golden 45s hanging from his shoulder straps spoke. "Mr. Miden is expecting you. Follow me."

Sydney thought, *Who is Miden?* She figured she must've heard the name wrong.

Walking up to the door, Sydney noticed a younger, biracial-looking girl getting into the back of a Rolls-Royce Phantom. She didn't think much of it.

When the front door swung open, to her surprise, it wasn't the older lady she had met before. It was a tall, sophisticated-looking guy standing in the doorway. He bore a striking resemblance to Ms.

Golden. He wore an all white Versace outfit with the shirt buttons undone. He looked to be in his early thirties.

He lowered his black and gold Versace glasses to get a better look at Sydney. "Wow, my mother told me you were beautiful. That's an understatement. You're gorgeous!" Miden said in a flirtatious type of way. Sydney smiled. In his own smooth way, you could tell he'd grown up in the States and had swagg.

They walked into the house to a large entrance filled with marble. They followed Miden into the living room where golden statues of Roman Emperors and Alpaca rugs filled the room. It was a nice house but had a real eighties vibe.

"I know you weren't expecting me. My name is Miden. Golden is my mother. She was busy, so she sent me. You can say I was curious about this woman I've been hearing so much about. I can say I'm not disappointed. Far as business, what was it you wanted to talk about?"

"Well, I just wanted to start paying off that debt." Sydney waved her hand at LA. He walked over with the duffle bag. "Two seventy," Sydney said, deciding to give the whole two seventy to the plug.

She thought the faster she could pay back the money that Omar had stolen, the sooner this nightmare would be over. One of the bodyguards grabbed the bag.

"Have you guys eaten anything yet? Let my chef whip you up something," Miden offered.

LA and Tasha began to follow the staff to the

kitchen. Miden reached out to grab Sydney's hand and said, "Let me show you something."

LA turned and started to follow Sydney, when the bodyguard stopped him. "Where she goes, I go," LA said, mean-mugging the bodyguard.

Sydney looked back at LA to reassure him she would be safe.

"You good, Boss Lady?" LA asked.

"I'm good."

Sydney was walking closely behind Miden, and behind her was the bodyguard from earlier. They walked into a room with over a half dozen naked women mixing and cutting piles of heroin. She couldn't believe what she was seeing.

"Why do this at your house?" Sydney asked.

"This isn't my house. It's just one of many stash spots for my family."

Miden walked Sydney into the next room where there were stacks of hundreds on the tables.

"See, my family can buy just about anything this world has to offer. However, the one thing we value more than money is loyalty. So when my mother told me everything that happened to you, I was surprised. You could've told the police who shot your husband but you didn't. Why?"

Sydney thought for a minute. She really didn't know why she didn't tell the police who shot Roc. "I don't know why."

Miden looked at her like she was a breath of fresh air. "Honest, as well. The more we talk, the more you amaze me." Miden walked Sydney to the kitchen where LA and Tasha were waiting.

"This shit so good, Girl. You need to try this," Tasha said, eating some food the chef had made.

LA wasn't eating. He was nervously waiting to leave as he leaned on the marble countertops. He was staying on point just in case the meeting didn't go right.

Sydney could tell Miden was flirting with her. She knew better than to mix business with pleasure – only if she could play it to her advantage.

"Miss, may I get you anything?" the chef asked.

Sydney looked down at her Rolex watch. "No, thank you." She then turned and said to Miden, "I have to be heading out."

"Why so soon? You haven't eaten anything."

"Yeah, I know, but I haven't seen my boys in weeks."

"Oh, okay. I understand. Let me walk you out."

Miden walked them out to the front door. As they were walking out the door, he reached out for a handshake and pulled her in closer to whisper in her ear.

"That problem ... you don't have to worry about that no more," Miden said.

Sydney looked confused, but she knew what that meant.

CHAPTER 10

Omar was still on the hunt for Sydney after coming up short at the house. He hit the streets hard, looking for her. He was driving through his old neighborhood and drove past the old house he grew up in. He had a flashback to when his mother killed his father.

"Bitch, I know whatchu did!" Orlando screamed at Monica.

"O, get the fuck outta the house!" Monica yelled back.

"Bitch, I ain't going no fucking where 'til you tell me what the fuck happened!"

Monica jumped up, pushing little Omar to the floor and reaching for her gun on the nightstand. Monica was always a hothead. She and Orlando had been playing this game since they were kids.

Big O was a stick-up artist. He would send Monica and her crew, the Wipeout Queens, to hit licks for him, but trouble came when Monica found out about another baby he was having with Tiffany. She was the complete opposite of Monica.

Tiffany was a nurse, a good girl. Once little Roc was born, O started to neglect Monica and Omar. So, Monica wanted her out of the picture. She had called her friend MeMe, who was a Wipeout Queen. "Aye, go get that bitch!" Monica had yelled on the phone. "Say less, Queen," MeMe responded.

The next night, Tiffany was leaving the hospital and walking towards the parking lot. A beautiful, darker-skinned woman walked up behind her wearing an eight-ball jacket and pulled out a gun.

Bang! Bang! Two shots to the back of the head.

When the bad news got back to Orlando, he broke down crying. He already knew who had done it. He rushed to Monica's house. When he got there, he kicked the door in.

"Bitch, where you at?!"

Monica was in her bedroom with little Omar.

"Bitch, why the fuck you go do that? You gone kill me now too? Come on then, Muthafucka! Shoot!"

She pointed the gun at Orlando's head. He was screaming and walking closer as baby Omar was crying. Suddenly, the gun went off. Bang!

Omar snapped back when he saw the police lights flashing in the rearview mirror.

"What the fuck the hook want?" Omar mumbled to himself. He wasn't tripping. His strap was in the stash spot. It was night outside, so he pulled over under the street light.

The tall White officer exited the squad car. *Tap.* Omar rolled the window down and handed the officer his license and registration.

"Mr. Williams, I'ma need you to step out of the car, please."

"What the fuck foe?" Omar mugged the officer before opening the door. "Officer, I don't understand why the fuck I need to get outta my car."

The officer was silent. He just walked Omar over by the squad car. "Spread your legs, Sir, and put your hands on the hood." The officer grabbed the handcuffs. When he reached for Omar's hands, Omar initially pulled away.

"Officer, why the fuck you arresting me? I know my rights!" Omar was yelling at the officer while he was putting the cuffs on Omar.

"Shut the fuck up, Monkey!" the officer said in a deep southern accent.

"What the fuck you call me, Bitch? I know my rights, Officer..." Omar paused to get the officer's name off his badge, "... Night. You don't have probable cause to arrest me!"

Night pushed Omar onto the backseat of the squad car and slammed the door shut.

"Muthafucka, I know my rights!"

Night jumped in the driver's seat of the squad car and grabbed his phone as Omar was yelling from the back seat.

"Shut up, Nigger!"

"I'ma sue the fuck outta your racist ass!"

Night made a call.

"Hello?" the receptionist answered. "How may I help you?"

"May I speak to Mr. Miden?"

"May I ask who's calling?"

"Officer Night."

"Hold please."

A couple of moments went by.

"Hello?"

"Mr. Miden, it's Night. I found that problem you were looking for."

"Uh, take him to the warehouse. I'll meet you there."

"Okay."

"Mr. Miden? Who the fuck is that? Aye, Man, let me the fuck outta here! You ain't no fucking police!" Omar screamed before kicking the back window.

That's when Night opened the window to the back seat. He grabbed Omar and stuck a needle in his arm.

"What the fuck is you doing? Let me the fuck go!" Omar felt himself getting tired. "W-what t-the fuck you do to me?" Omar passed out in the back seat.

"That a shut your ass up," Night said, pulling off.

Sydney pulled up to Tasha's ma's house to visit the boys. She knocked on the door, and Rocko opened the door.

"Ma!" Rocko shouted in excitement, seeing his mother. He squeezed her as hard as he could.

Ms. Jackson walked in from the back room, yelling at Rocko, "Who the hell told your little bad ass to open the door?"

"Ms. Jackson, it's Ma."

"I don't care who it is. You don't open no doors in my house. Hey, Sydney, where is that no good ass daughter of mine at?"

"She dropped me off at the hospital. I think she went back home," Sydney replied.

Ms. Jackson just stared smugly at her.

Ms. Jackson was seventy years old. You could tell she would be someone who had pink rollers in her hair, with a dirty housecoat on, and with a Bible nearby.

"When you gone find a good man to raise these boys with, because you girls pick these no-good-ass niggas that end up leaving y'all foe prison or the graveyard. I'm glad Lilly's not here. She's probably rolling in her grave." She turned and left the room with a shake of her head.

Lilly was Sydney's mother. She and Ms. Jackson had been friends and had gone to the same church. Sydney wasn't surprised at Ms. Jackson's comments. She and Tasha had been hearing it since they were kids. Sydney just shook her head.

Rocky ran into the room after hearing his mom's voice. He jumped all on Sydney. "Ma, I missed you! We going home?"

She could see the excitement in their faces, thinking she was there to bring them home. "Not just yet. I still got things to work out before y'all come home."

She could see the expression change on their

faces. To help lift their spirit, she went on to tell them how she was trying to make some positive things happen for them so they didn't have to worry about anything again.

Beep! Sydney's phone went off. It was a text from an unknown number. She read the text. It was from Miden, and he was telling her to meet him at this address. Sydney sighed and turned to look at the boys once more.

Rocko and Rocky were looking as if they were about to cry. Sydney called Ms. Jackson back into the room.

"Aye, Ms. Jackson, I'ma need you to watch the boys a little longer, please." Sydney reached for her purse and pulled out a stack of money. "This is for you, Ms. Jackson, for watching the boys."

Ms. Jackson took the money and stuffed it in her bra. "Well, thank you for the money, but when you coming to get they bad asses?"

"Soon. I just need to take care of a few things at the house before they come home."

"Okay, these boys already don't have they father. They need they mother."

"I know, Ms. Jackson. Boys, I have to go. Come give me a kiss before I leave."

They looked disappointed that they weren't going home. Sydney rushed out the door, wondering why Miden wanted to meet so soon already.

CHAPTER 11

Sydney approached what looked like an abandoned warehouse. She wondered why he would want to meet here. As she pulled up to the warehouse, she took note of the rolled-up door. She saw a police car next to a white S550 parked inside. Sydney couldn't make out the faces. They were too far away.

One of the guys waved their hands, signaling her to come over to them. She parked and cautiously got out. The closer she got, the more she could make out the faces of the people. She noticed Miden talking to a police officer. Once she finally made it over by them, she saw it was Officer Night.

That's the same officer who pulled us over, she thought to herself.

Miden gave a signal, and Night walked over to his squad car and opened the back door.

"Come on, Big Boy. Getcha ass outta here."

"What the fuck!" Sydney screamed, seeing Omar dragged out the back seat of the police car. "What's going on, Miden?" Sydney mumbled.

"What do you think?" Miden responded.

She knew exactly what was happening, but she

didn't respond vocally. She just shook her head.

"See, my family values loyalty, but to be a member of my family, you have to be willing to give your life as well as take a life." After Miden said that, he pulled a golden 45 out of his shoulder strap under his Gucci suit jacket and handed it to Sydney. "Show me you're ready."

She knew what he meant.

Omar was slowly regaining consciousness. "W-what t-the f-fuck?" he mumbled.

Omar couldn't make out the people standing over him. He could hear somebody talking but couldn't understand what they were saying.

His head was still foggy from whatever Night drugged him with. Once his vision came back, he saw Sydney standing over him holding a gun.

"What the fuck?" Omar started laughing. "Oh, it's you. Damn, I ain't see this coming. Bitch, you surprised me. I should've killed yo' ass at the house."

"Shut the fuck up, Omar!" Sydney yelled. She was shaking so much that she almost dropped the gun.

Miden grabbed her hands. "You got this. Your first time is always going to be the hardest," he said to ease her mind.

"I can't do this!"

"Yes, you can. He's the reason you're here in the first place. It's because of him that your kids don't have their father."

Sydney was crying, "I can't! I can't!"

"Bitch, just do it already. I rather it be you than one of these jet-set-lookin' muthafuckas or this cock-suckin' ass pig!" Omar shouted.

Sydney slowly pointed the gun at Omar's head. "I'm sorry!"

"Whatchu sorry foe? I'ma gangsta. Whatchu think … I'ma beg for my life? Y'all ain't shit!" Omar screamed out.

The gun got heavier as Sydney cried. That's when Omar yelled, "Bitch, come on!"

Bang! The gun went off. Miden grabbed Sydney's hands, trying to calm her down. He slowly grabbed the gun from her hands. She was frozen in fear after seeing Omar's lifeless body slumped over with blood pouring from his head.

This was the first time she had taken a life. She started throwing up.

"Allll … damn. She throwing up on my boots!" Night yelled as the bodyguards laughed.

"I'm sorry!" she said, crying.

"Bitch, fuck your sorrys," Night responded.

Miden slapped Night. "Shut you fucking mouth with that. Now, apologize to her!"

"I'm sorry, Ma'am," Night said, looking at the ground in fear for his life.

Miden carried Sydney over to the back seat of his S550. Once she got in the back seat, she passed right out.

◆ ◆ ◆

Later the next day, Sydney woke up in somebody else's bed with clothes on that weren't hers.

Confused, she started to panic.

When she got out of the bed, she noticed the bedroom doorknob turning. Before the door could open, she hid under the bed. She could see somebody walking into the room.

"Sydney?" somebody yelled out. "Where the hell she go?"

She recognized the voice as she slowly crawled from under the bed. "Miden?" Sydney said back.

"Yeah. Whatchu doing under the bed?" Miden responded.

"Where am I?"

"You're at my house."

"What am I doing here? And how did I get here?" she asked, looking confused.

"I drove you here."

"Wait. Why can't I remember?"

"You passed out before we left the warehouse."

She suddenly had a flashback of Omar's lifeless body slumped over on the floor of the warehouse. "Oh my God!" Remembering what she had done, she looked as if she was about to throw up again.

"Look, there is nothing we can do about that. It's the past, so leave it there," Miden said to assure her that he had her back. "Your clothes had to be washed. They're in the closet. I came to check on you and bring you extra towels, in case you need them. The bathroom is behind that door." Miden handed her the towels he was carrying.

"Thank you," Sydney smiled. She felt safe being with Miden. She was still shaken up about Omar because it was still on her mind.

As she was walking into the bathroom, Miden was beginning to leave. While she was quickly getting undressed, she forgot to shut the door.

Miden walked in; he had forgotten to tell her where to meet him after her shower. He was surprised to see Sydney already standing there naked. He stared at her, unable to catch his breath. Sydney was gorgeous, like the tattoo read on her lower back.

She wasn't bothered by him staring. She was actually turned on. She slowly leaned in through the shower glass door to turn the shower on, showing off her gorgeous waxed body and beautiful curves. *I just need something to take my mind off Omar,* she thought to herself. She decided to use Miden. She stepped through the shower glass door and looked at Miden.

"You just gone stare or are you coming to join me?" she asked.

He undressed at the door and walked in. As the water ran down her back, he moved in closer. He moved her long blonde hair off her back slowly and softly kissed her neck.

"O-oh!" Sydney moaned softly as he grabbed her neck tightly. She reached behind her back, grabbing his dick slowly and stroking him. After she turned around to get a good look at him, she knelt down while still stroking him. She kissed the tip of his dick before slowly licking and sucking it. He moaned.

"Whose is it?" she asked.

"It's … uh … all yours, Baby!" he responded. Then, he grunted, "Y-yes!"

Minutes later, she wiped her bottom lip while she caught her breath, holding onto the shower walls. When she came back up, Miden pushed her against the wall, licking and biting her pink, pierced nipples. Spreading her legs apart, he began massaging her clit. He rubbed his dick between her legs.

"You want this dick?"

"Y-yes!" Sydney responded.

Miden flipped her around and ran his dick up and down her pussy. He could feel how hot she was. As she moaned, he pushed himself against her, forcing every inch of himself inside her.

As he pushed harder and harder, she screamed out in pleasure, "Oh shit, Daddy! It feels so good!"

Miden eventually whispered in Sydney's ear, "Oh, I'm about to cum!"

Sydney pulled away before he could cum in her. She took a minute to get her breath before hearing him speak again.

"Oh … shit … damn, that was great…. When you get done, get dressed and come to the kitchen. I got a surprise for you," Miden said then walked out of the shower.

That's when she noticed the large sabre tattoo on his back. Sydney knew she had made a mistake having sex with Miden. She didn't want that to affect their business.

A while later, Sydney walked back into the bedroom. Lying on the bed was a black Chanel dress with a Chanel shoe box next to it. She just smiled as she tried on the dress and heels. Miden walked back into the room in a Tom Ford suit and with a Richard Mille watch on.

"Wow, you're gorgeous! Do the dress and heels fit well?"

"Yeah. How do you know what size I wear?" Sydney asked.

"My tailor guessed. I'm glad it fits. Do you like?"

"Y-yes, thank you. I can see you clean up nice too," she said, smiling. "What time is it?" she asked, wondering if she had time to visit Roc. She felt guilty about her and Miden.

He looked down at his Richard Mille watch. "Five-thirty. You've been out of it for a while, given the shock. Why?"

"No reason. This is a nice house. Do you stay here alone?"

"No, it's just one of the many properties we own."

As they walked through the home, the luxury condo layout was nice. It even had the smell of new furniture. There was an older Latina lady standing next to the chef she'd met before. Miden and Sydney walked over to the dining room table, where the Latina lady pulled out their chairs.

"This is my personal chef, Tony. He's a great chef, and this is Sofia. She cleans the apartment," Miden informed Sydney.

Chef Tony bowed then presented them with two plates of food. "I hope you enjoy," Chef Tony said and smiled before walking away.

Miden grabbed the box Sofia was now holding. She then disappeared as well. "I told you I had a gift for you," Miden said to Sydney with that charming ass swagg.

"I thought my gift was the dress and heels?" Sydney replied in confusion. Miden handed her the gift box. "What's this?" she asked. She then opened the box and saw a set of car keys with the initials *RR* inscribed on it. "What's this foe?" she asked.

"Your new car," Miden responded.

"A new car?" she asked, surprised. "Are you crazy? Why would you give me a new car?" Sydney was staring at him in shock.

"My family has an image to uphold in these streets and you're a member of that family now, so you represent us." Miden reached into his pocket and pulled out another set of keys.

"And what are these foe?"

"Your new place."

"Wait … What are you talking about? What new place?"

Miden started looking around the upscale apartment with a smile on his face. "You're looking at it. This is all yours now. Sofia will help with the cleaning, and Chef Tony will cook for you and the boys."

Sydney did her best to keep her composure. She was overjoyed to hear the good news, thinking she was able now to bring her boys home.

"Thank you so much. I can never repay you for this."

Miden leaned in and whispered, "You are so beautiful and amazing – and stronger than you realize. You make me want to put you on this table and do some incredible shit to you."

Sydney's eyebrow rose at the comment.

Miden just started laughing with a regrettable look on his face, then said, "Yeah, I would love nothing more, but…."

He stopped and sighed before finishing, "Believe me, I wish I didn't have to conduct business today; however, we all have an obligation to the family."

Sydney just watched Miden as he headed out the door. She felt relief, even though his ass was fine, handsome, and apparently, rich as hell. *I gotta learn this damn game and stay ahead of it,* Sydney contemplated.

CHAPTER 12

Damn! I can't believe it, she thought to herself as Chef Tony later walked back in and over to her to pick up the plates from the table.

Sofia, who was wiping off the table, said, "Ms. Williams, there is something in the closet for you."

"Huh? What is it?" Sydney asked.

"I don't know. Mr. Miden instructed me to let you know after he'd left."

"What closet is it?"

"It's in the master bedroom."

Sydney thought she'd just left the master bedroom. "Where is that room at?"

"It's around the corner in the back."

Sydney started walking through the house to look for the closet, when she noticed a large window. She looked out in surprise at how high in the air the apartment was.

"Damn, this shit high as a muthafucka." When she finally made it to the master bedroom, she opened the door - amazed at how big the room was. She walked over to the closet door and was surprised to see the duffle bag she had left over at Miden's stash house.

She wondered if that was the surprise. She unzipped the bag. It was the two seventy she had given Miden to pay off her debt and a note from Ms. Golden.

"My son was very impressed with you - so much so that he wanted to make you a member of my family. Loyalty is valued much higher than money in this family, so all debts will be forgiven. Welcome to the family."

Sydney burst into tears, thinking her nightmare was finally over. She called Sofia, the maid.

"*Si*, what can I do for you?" Sofia asked.

"Have you seen my phone?"

"*Si*, Mr. Miden threw it away."

"What the fuck? All my information was in there."

Sofia reached into her pocket, pulled out a brand new iPhone and handed it to Sydney.

She grabbed it, looking confused. "What's this foe?"

"It's your new phone. All your information from the old phone is in this one."

"Why can't I use my old phone?"

"Because this phone can't be traced or tapped."

Sydney just nodded her head. She started thinking about everything that had happened, from Omar to Miden. That's when she remembered visiting hours were almost over at the hospital.

If she wanted to visit Roc, she had to leave now. She grabbed her things and swung open the front door, bumping into a large bodyguard who was waiting in the hallway.

"Excuse me," Sydney said, losing her balance and falling to the floor.

"No problem," the large bodyguard said, pulling her to her feet. "My name is Mark. I'm your bodyguard. Mr. Miden wants me with you 24/7. Is there anywhere I can drive you?"

She didn't ponder on this because she needed to get to the hospital fast. "I need to make it to the hospital before visiting hours are over."

Mark nodded and started walking towards the elevator doors. He pushed the button to the lowest level floor, and they got off at the garage. There weren't that many cars in the garage. Looking at the ones that were there, they were very nice cars.

Sydney followed Mark through the garage, looking for her truck. That's when Mark pulled out a set of Rolls-Royce keys from his front pocket. "Here you go, Ma'am."

All of a sudden, it hit her, and she remembered Miden had bought her a new car. It was a white Rolls-Royce Ghost. Mark opened the back door, and Sydney got in the car, looking around like a kid in a candy store.

It was her first time having something this nice. She had other nice things but never *this* nice. As they drove off, she decided to call Tasha on her new phone.

"Hello!" Sydney said into her phone.

"Who the fuck is dis?"

"Bitch, yo' sister. Who you think?"

Tasha paused for a minute since she didn't see the phone number flash. "Sydney? Bitch, is that you?"

"Yeah, T. You thought it was one of them bitches who niggas you be fuckin'?"

Tasha laughed. "Girl, who phone you calling from? I been calling you all day."

"Bitch, it's a long ass story. I'll tell you later. You ain't gone believe this shit."

"Oh yeah? What happened?" Tasha asked with interest.

"I'll call you later. You talk to LA?"

"Yeah. He been blowing my phone up, looking for you."

Sydney just shook her head. "Tell him I'll call later."

"Bitch, *you* call that little nigga."

"T, just tell him – damn!"

Tasha smacked her lips. "Yeah, okay."

"Love you, Sis!"

"Love you too."

Sydney ended the call. Pulling up at the hospital, Sydney started feeling nervous about visiting Roc. After the bodyguard opened the door, Sydney started walking up to the front desk.

"Mrs. Williams," the receptionist called out. "Hey, that's a beautiful dress."

"Thank you. Visiting hours isn't over, is it?"

"Naw, you made it in time. I'm glad you got somebody with you this time," the receptionist said, looking up at the bodyguard. "Here's your visitor's pass. Have a good one."

Sydney grabbed the pass and rushed over to the elevators to make her visit with Roc. Although she was still nervous about this visit, she couldn't help but be happy for getting herself from under Ms. Golden's and Omar's controls.

As she walked off the elevator and headed towards Roc's room, she overheard the nurses talking about a body that had been found in the middle of the street with no head.

"Excuse me, I don't mean to be in your business, but *what* happened today on the news?" Sydney asked.

"Girl, they been talking about that shit all day on the news. Look, they talking about it now," the nurse said, grabbing the remote from the desk. She turned up the volume on the TV.

"Breaking News: We are still reporting on the headless body found on the Westside of Detroit. My sources are telling me that the victim's name was Omar Williams. The detectives on the case believe it was a gang hit by the Triads," the news anchor reported.

Sydney's eyes went wide when she heard Omar's name on the TV. "Oh my God," she breathed. Sydney started stumbling from the nurse's desk.

"Are you okay, Ma'am?" the nurse asked Sydney as Mark was helping her to get steady on her feet.

"Yeah, I'm good, just a little dehydrated," Sydney responded. The nurse handed Sydney some water to drink. "Thank you. I'm okay now."

Once Sydney got herself back together, she resumed walking towards Roc's room, thinking about what she had just heard. When she finally made it to the room, she slowly turned the doorknob. Right before the door opened, the hospital staff paged her over the speaker.

"Paging a Sydney Williams to the front desk."

She looked confused at Mark, wondering what was going on. They walked back to the nurse's desk.

"Someone paged a Sydney Williams?" she asked.

"Oh yeah, you have a call," the staff member said.

Sydney looked up at Mark with that same confused look on her face, but Mark looked just as confused as she was. The nurse handed her the phone.

"Hello?" Sydney said.

"So you the bitch who killed my son?" the voice said.

"What?!" Sydney said, looking around. "Who is dis?" she questioned.

"The last bitch you ever hear from." *Click!* The person on the phone hung up.

"Hello! Hello!" Sydney screamed into the telephone.

Ding. The elevator door opened, and a woman with a black hoodie on walked off the elevator - opening fire at Sydney. *Bang! Bang! Bang!*

Mark grabbed Sydney, pulled his gun and started firing back at ol' girl while running towards the fire exit with Sydney.

"Damn! What the fuck! Who the fuck is that bitch?" Mark asked Sydney.

"I don't fucking know!" she responded.

They ran down the fire staircase, making it to the lobby where the receptionist and security guard were dead. As they ran out the door to the parking lot, a black truck pulled up fast, burning tire rubber. Two females jumped out shooting up the cars, trying to hit Sydney and Mark. Mark was "blowing" back and ducking behind the cars while pushing Sydney's head down.

"Stay down! Who the fuck are these bitches?" Mark was yelling as bullets were flying past their heads. The car windows shattered, and glass fell all over Sydney's head.

"Give me one of your guns!" Sydney yelled at Mark.

"Fuck! Damn! … Here!" Mark handed one of his 45s. "We need to make it to the car. You run; I'll cover you!" Mark said, looking at Sydney and trying to get her focused.

"Okay!" Sydney said.

Kneeling down, she slowly crept to the back of the car. When one of the females spotted her and started shooting right above her head, Mark saw Sydney was pinned down. Mark jumped out to help her and started bustin' at ol' girl. *Bang! Bang!* He hit her in the neck and she fell.

Mark yelled, "Get the fuck outta here!"

Sydney took off running towards her white Ghost. The other girl was reloading as Sydney was getting into the driver's seat. Sydney started the car up and pulled off to grab Mark, who was still shooting at the other girl.

"Come on, get in the car!" Sydney screamed out, pushing the passenger door open.

He jumped in, still shooting as they were pulling away. The girl was still shooting back at the bulletproof Ghost. Right before Mark could close the door, a bullet struck him in the shoulder.

"Aw! Shit! Fuck!" Mark yelled out as the car swerved out the parking lot. "Damn, what the fuck is going on?" he said, doing his best to stop the bleeding from his arm.

"Where are we going?! Should I take you to another hospital or something?!" Sydney asked in a panic, swerving in and out of traffic.

Beep! Beep! They heard cars blowing at them.

"Slow the fuck down! Call Miden!" Mark yelled, still bleeding all over Sydney's new white Rolls-Royce seats.

Sydney called the phone number that Mark rattled off.

"Hello?" Miden answered.

"Mark's been shot!" Sydney screamed to Miden.

"Wait! Wait! Slow down. I can't hear you clearly," Miden said.

"Three women ambushed us at the hospital. Mark was shot in the shoulder. I think he's bleeding out!" Sydney said, looking over at Mark while driving. She thought Mark was going to die. She did her best to keep him awake because she could tell he was slowly fading off.

"Stay up! Come on – fight! We almost at another hospital!" she screamed at Mark.

"Sydney, take him to the safe house!" Miden said. He heard Sydney crying uncontrollably. "Calm down. Everything is going to be alright," Miden said calmly to calm her down. "I'm sending you the address."

Beep! Sydney got the message from Miden. She proceeded to the address where Miden wanted them to meet him.

CHAPTER 13

Sydney pulled in fast, almost hitting the house on Joy Rd and Franklin. When she jumped out the car, she rushed over to Mark and swung open the passenger door. Mark dropped his 45 Smith & Wesson out the car onto the ground.

Sydney yelled out for help. Two large men rushed out the door and grabbed Mark, carrying him into the house. Sydney followed and cleared a few items from the bed so the two men could lay Mark on it.

Seconds later, Miden pulled into the driveway with a woman wearing scrubs. They rushed into the house. The five-foot-two-inch blonde White woman pushed the two large men out the way so she could cut Mark's clothes off. She started to pull IVs and surgical equipment out of her bag.

"What is she doing? We need to take him to the hospital!" Sydney screamed.

Miden grabbed Sydney, pulling her to the side. "She knows what she's doing. Calm down and tell me everything that happened."

"I don't know what happened," Sydney said, throwing her head back and crying.

"Start at the beginning when y'all left the house,"

he coached her.

She took a deep breath. "Mark was taking me to the hospital to visit my husband. Just as we approached the room, the hospital staff paged me and told me I had a phone call. When I answered, some bitch told me I was the one who killed her son. I asked who dis was, and that's when some girl came off the elevator bustin' at us. Them bitches were everywhere. If it wasn't foe Mark, I would be dead right now."

Miden shook his head and hugged Sydney to let her know she was safe now. "Everything is going to be okay. I'll figure this shit out. Whoever took a shot at you, took a shot at me, so sleep easy. They won't make it through next week."

Sydney's car was shot up with dings, so Miden decided to take her home. "Come on. Let me take you home," he told her.

When they walked outside, there was a fleet of cars and armed bodyguards waiting for them. Miden walked Sydney over to the black S550 Benz and opened the door. After one of the bodyguards opened Miden's door, he jumped into the backseat with Sydney. They pulled off, being followed by a fleet of cars and bodyguards.

"What about Mark? Is he going to make it?" Sydney asked Miden, worried about Mark's well-being.

"Of course! He is a tough guy. Don't worry."

They pulled into the apartment parking garage, where even more security guards were waiting.

Sydney walked into the apartment and moved straight for her bedroom. She threw her clothes off and hopped in the shower. As the water was running down her body, Mark's blood began to wash from her.

That's when Miden got in the shower behind her, holding onto her as she started to cry. She was overcome with emotions. She turned around, and that's when he noticed her crying. As he wiped her tears from her eyes, she felt understood and taken care of.

She softly kissed him and walked out the shower, not bothering to cover herself. She walked out to the bed. Miden followed her to the bedroom.

He pushed her onto the bed, and they started making passionate love with each other. After they were done, Sydney fell asleep on top of Miden's chest.

The next morning, she was woken up by the sun rising through the window. When she rolled over, she noticed Miden wasn't in the bed. The smell of bacon and eggs being cooked was in the air. She climbed out of the bed and left the room.

"Miden, is that you?" Sydney yelled out, walking towards the kitchen.

"*Hola*, Ms. Williams. How can I help you?" Sofia, the maid, asked.

"Where is Miden?"

"Mr. Miden had business to attend to. Is there anything I can do for you?"

"Did he say how long he was going to be gone?"

"No, he just instructed me to tell you he would be

back later."

"Okay, thank you." Sydney started walking back towards the bedroom.

"Ms. Williams, do you want me to bring the food back to the room?"

"Yeah, that would be fine," Sydney responded. She jumped back into the bed, grabbing the remote to turn on Fox News.

"Breaking News Update: There was a shootout at Detroit Receiving Hospital, where two nurses were shot, and a receptionist and security guard were killed. There was also a suspect killed at the scene of the crime. We just received information about the suspects in this crime.

My sources are telling me that the suspect killed at the hospital was Angel Flowers. She is a known member of a gang called Wipeout Queens.

The other suspect captured on video camera is a Sydney Williams.

Detectives are looking for her in the questioning of the Detroit hospital shooting. If you have any information, please call 1-800-CRIME-STOPPERS."

Sydney's phone started ringing. She jumped nervously after hearing that the police were looking for her about the murders at the hospital.

"Hello?" Sydney answered shakily.

"Bitch, what the fuck is going on? I'm here watching the news, and your face is all over it. They talking about you had something to do with them murders at the hospital!"

Sydney started crying. "I don't know what the

fuck is going on. I was on my way to visit Roc, and some bitches got to bustin' at me. They almost killed me, T!"

"Damn, Girl. I didn't know all that shit was going on. Do you even know these bitches?"

"I don't know who these hoes is!" Sydney was so stressed that her mind was as cloudy as the sky.

"The news lady said one of them was in a gang called the Wipeout Queens. You ain't never heard of that shit?"

Sydney started thinking about where she'd heard that name from. "I don't remember, but it sounds familiar though."

"I'm about to hit da streets and find out who these bitches are. I'll let you know when I get something. Stay safe. Love you, Sis."

"Love you too."

CHAPTER 14

Knock! Knock! Knock!

"Damn, who da fuck knockin' at my door like da police?" LA swung open the door. "Tasha, why the fuck you bangin' on my door like da police? It's early as shit."

Tasha pushed her way past LA inside the house. "Nigga, because I been calling you all day. Where da fuck is yo' phone?"

"It's dead after trying to call Sydney all yesterday."

A girl walked in from the bedroom, just wearing a t-shirt. She looked to be in her early twenties and had strikingly beautiful, clear, dark skin. Apparently, LA also liked his women thick as hell. "LA, is everything good?" the girl asked.

"Bitch, if it wasn't, what the fuck you gone do?" Tasha mean-mugged the girl.

"Bitch, whatchu mean what I'm gone do!" the girl yelled back, walking towards Tasha.

LA stepped in between 'em. "Man, chill the fuck out! Dianne, take yo' ass back in da room." She rolled her eyes and stomped back to the room. "What the fuck do you want, Tasha?"

"Nigga, I'm not here foe you! I'm here foe Sydney."

"You talked to her?"

"Yeah, and she in trouble with the police! They looking foe her."

"Wait ... What da fuck foe?"

"Nigga, dat shit is all over da news! They saying she had something to do with the shootout at Detroit Receiving Hospital."

"Fuck naw!"

"Yeah, I know."

LA sat down on the couch, throwing his hands on his head in disbelief about what Tasha had just said.

"Have you talked to her since then?" he asked.

"Yeah."

"What she say happened?" LA jumped off of the couch and asked aggressively.

"She don't really know what happened. She just told me she was at the hospital to visit Roc, when some bitches started bustin' at her."

"Who the fuck is these hoes?"

"She don't know. All we know is what the news anchor said - that one of 'em was in a gang called the Wipeout Queens. That's why I'm here. You ain't never heard of that shit?"

"Yeah, that's them old bitches that used to be putting plays down on niggas back in the day. Why the fuck would they have a problem with Sydney?"

"I don't know but we need to find out."

Dianne was listening in the back room to Tasha

and LA.

Little did they know her older sister was a Wipeout Queen. She pulled her phone out and called her sister.

"What up doe, Lil Sis? I'm a little busy. Is it important?"

"MeMe, you know that girl you looking foe?"

"Dianne, that ain't yo' business."

Dianne smacked her lips. "Naw, listen. I been fucking with this nigga named LA. I'm over this nigga house right now, and some bitch come in here screaming about her friend Sydney being all over the news for that shootout at Detroit Receiving Hospital."

"What's the nigga name?"

"LA!"

"Text me the address and keep 'em there. Be safe, Little Sis."

"Okay."

Right as LA walked into the room, Dianne was hanging up the phone. "Aye, Ma, I gotta take care of something. Let yourself out. I'll getchu later," LA said, walking towards the door.

Dianne grabbed LA's hand, pulling him in closer. After she took his middle finger and placed it in her mouth, she started to slowly suck on it. All the while, she was trying to undo his pants.

He pulled away from her. "Look, Ma, I got to go!"

"Damn, Nigga, so you gone play me foe dat bitch?" Dianne said, rolling her neck.

"Look, Bitch, it ain't like that. Now get cho' shit

and get the fuck outta my crib." LA grabbed her by the arm, pulling her through the house towards the front door. Tasha moved out the way, pointing her finger at Dianne and laughing.

"Bitch, fuck you and this hoe-ass nigga!" Dianne yelled at Tasha.

"Yeah, okay," LA said, throwing her out the front door.

"Nigga, you gone regret this shit. Watch what I say!" Dianne said, kicking the front door after LA slammed it in her face. Tasha was still laughing at LA.

"You see what the fuck I go through?" LA said.

"Nigga, don't complain now. You wasn't when she was giving you some pussy. Learn how to control yo' hoes!" Tasha said, mugging LA.

"Mann … Shut da fuck up and come on," LA said, frustrated and walking out the door behind Tasha.

LA and Tasha didn't know it, but Dianne was following close behind them in her car. She called her sister MeMe.

"Hello?" MeMe answered.

"Aye, Sis, they left the house."

"I told yo' ass to keep that nigga there! Fuck! Where dat nigga go?"

"He in the car with ol' girl. I'm following them down Jefferson, heading downtown."

"Alright, stay on 'em and don't lose 'em! Send me your location."

A few minutes later, *Beep!* MeMe's phone went off. It was the location where Dianne was. "Okay, I see you," MeMe mumbled.

LA and Tasha were pulling up to some high-end apartment complex. Right before they had left the house, Sydney sent Tasha a text with the address to where she was at.

"Who place is dis?" LA asked.

"Shit, Boy, I don't know. She just sent me an address and told me to come over asap. She had something to tell me."

Pulling into the parking lot, they could see a line of security guards.

"Who the fuck stay here – the President?" LA said as he stared at all the security guards, who all had AR-15s.

As they parked, armed men rushed the car and pulled both of them out of the car. "Aye, Nigga, let me the fuck go!" LA said, pushing the security off of him.

One of the guards' radio went off. "They good! Let them up!" somebody yelled through the radio. The guards let them go.

LA and Tasha were confused, walking over to the elevator. They didn't know what had just happened. Tasha looked over at LA and said, "That was Sydney on the radio." LA looked at her like she was trippin'.

All the while, Dianne was parked across the street with a good view of everything. She had watched the whole thing unfold.

MeMe pulled up beside Dianne's car. She rolled down her window.

"What's up, Lil Sis? Where that nigga at?" MeMe asked.

"Him and ol' girl just jumped on the elevator. Shit hot though, Sis. They got all type of security."

MeMe pulled her hoodie off, revealing how bad she was. She was in her late forties, but she didn't look it. She was gorgeous, with milk-chocolate smooth skin and long jet black hair. She looked like that Instagram model Bernice Burgos.

MeMe turned and tapped her friend on the shoulder. "You see that shit, Red?"

"Yeah, them niggas strapped the fuck up. We gone need all the Queens foe dis shit." MeMe just nodded and made the call.

LA and Tasha got off the elevator. When they got to the apartment door, LA started knocking. He nervously waited, not knowing what to expect on the other side of the door. The doorknob slowly turned.

As four car loads of Wipeout Queens were pulling up outside, MeMe and Red got out the car and walked towards the other members. A female wearing a bulletproof vest got out holding two AR-15s. She handed them over to Red and MeMe.

"Look, Queens, this shit for Queen Monica and little Omar. I want that bitch dead – straight up. LONG LIVE THE QUEEN!" MeMe shouted.

"LONG LIVE THE QUEEN!" the crew of females shouted back as they all started walking towards the apartments ....

TO BE CONTINUED.....

EPILOGUE

Life changes in a minute. Just when you think you're riding high, shit happens. And as we say in "The D", that's *fa' sho'*!

Can Sydney survive what's coming - from the streets *and* from the law?

In *Detroit City Girls - Part II*, the real showdown begins!

ACKNOWLEDGEMENTS

Thank you to all of those who have supported me through this project. I appreciate you more than you know.

ABOUT THE AUTHOR

Kita Cochran

Kita Cochran is a Detroit, Michigan native. Her literary work reflects the many sides of her complex metropolitan city - including its grit, its hustle culture and its love of beautiful things.